ROXY

THE LAST UNISAURUS REX

WRITTEN BY
EVA CHEN

ILLUSTRATED BY
MATTHEW RIVERA

FEIWEL AND FRIENDS · NEW YORK

A FEIWEL AND FRIENDS BOOK
An imprint of Macmillan Publishing Group, LLC
120 Broadway, New York, NY 10271

ROXY, THE LAST UNISAURUS REX
Copyright © 2020 by Eva Chen. All rights reserved.
Printed in China by RR Donnelley Asia Printing Solutions Ltd.,
Dongguan City, Guangdong Province

Our books may be purchased in bulk for promotional,
educational, or business use. Please contact your local
bookseller or the Macmillan Corporate and Premium
Sales Department at (800) 221-7945 ext. 5442 or by
email at MacmillanSpecialMarkets@macmillan.com.

Library of Congress Cataloging-in-Publication Data is available.
ISBN 978-1-250-61992-1 (hardcover)

Book design by Carol Ly
Feiwel and Friends logo designed by Filomena Tuosto
First edition, 2020

10 9 8 7 6 5 4 3 2 1

mackids.com

To Ren and all the kids out there who love dinosaurs AND unicorns. Don't ever change.

My name is Roxy and I'm the absolutely, completely, and totally LAST Unisaurus Rex in the world.

Excuse me?
You've never HEARD of a Unisaurus Rex?

Well, it's only the most magical creature in the world.

Half Dinosaur, half Unicorn. UNISAURUS!

And the Rex? Well, my mom was a Tyrannosaurus Rex.

I got my
gorgeous smile
from my mom . . .

As well as my extremely
healthy appetite . . .

ROAR

And my **slight** anger issues . . .

But this glorious mane?

And this runway-ready prance?

And this SPARKLE?

DADDY'S GIRL

It's all from my dad!

My teachers tell me how great it is to be
ONE IN A MILLION!

A SINGULAR SENSATION!

But can I tell you a secret?

Get a little closer . . .

closer . . .

Too close?

Sometimes it's lonely being one of a kind.

At school, the Stegosauruses have seesaw buddies.

The Pterodactyls get to use a tandem bike.

And the Diplodocuses always have tennis partners.

But everything's going to change today. I'm on a mission.

A mission to find a
BEST FRIEND.

Hello, my fellow horned friends!
Can I join you for lunch?

Girl, unless you have
three horns, you can't sit with us.

Oooh, are you guys having a race?

Can I join you?

Hey, guys! Slow down!

I said, **HEY!**

Well, you look like
a friendly bunch!
Can I join your squad?

Can I get an N?

Can I get an O?

Hi!

Oh, never mind.

Hi! What's that on your head?

A horn, of course.

What's this wavy stuff?

It's my mane!
I brush it sixteen
times a day.

You're just too much,
Roxy Rex.

You'll never be one of us.

Where do I belong?

Say, you look like you
need a friend.

Leave me alone,
I'm too busy being lonely.

I can see that. But, uh, you know . . .
I've never met another Dinocorn.

A WHAT?

A Dinocorn!

Well, I'm a Brontocorn to be specific—my dad's a Brontosaurus and my mom's a Unicorn.

I've never heard
of a Brontocorn.

Really? The first thing you need to
know is that we live by a delicious
vegetarian diet. I eat lots of leafy
greens! Want some kale salad?

Um, can I have a side
of steak with that?

Brontocorns are calm, gentle creatures.

I meditate every day . . .

Ommmm . . .

Where's the rest
of your pack?

Well, there's only one of me.
I am what they call
ONE OF A KIND.

No way! Me too!

What do you say WE start our
own pack? After all, we Dinocorns
have to stick together.

What do you say
to a game of tennis?
Or the seesaw?
Or a tandem bike ride?

I'm so glad to have a friend like you.

DINO MITE!

Meet Roxy and all of her dinosaur friends!

Archaeopteryx
This small, winged dinosaur is widely considered to be the earliest known bird.

Brontocorn
Half prancing Unicorn, half veggie-loving Brontosaurus—and completely awesome!

Diplodocus
This giant, gentle, long-necked vegetarian is closely related to the Brontosaurus.

Pterodactyl
Swoosh! These flying reptiles could have wingspans of up to twenty-three feet.

Spinosaurus
This massive meat eater's main accessory? A giant sail-like fin on its spine!

Stegosaurus
This dino is roughly the size of a school bus and known for having huge protective plates on its back.

Triceratops
The *tri* in triceratops refers to this dinosaur's three horns on its head—which also sports a birdlike beak and a frill around its neck.

Tyrannosaurus Rex
The carnivore tyrant lizard king may have been humongous, but it had teeny, tiny arms.

Unisaurus Rex
Half sparklelicious Unicorn, half ferocious Tyrannosaurus Rex—100% superstar!

Velociraptor
With a name that means *speedy thief*, this dino is known for being small, ultra-fast, and ferociously clawed.